Dear Parents:

Congratulations! Your child is taking the first steps on an exciting journey. The destination? Independent reading!

STEP INTO READING® will help your child get there. The program offers five steps to reading success. Each step includes fun stories and colorful art or photographs. In addition to original fiction and books with favorite characters, there are Step into Reading Non-Fiction Readers, Phonics Readers and Boxed Sets, Sticker Readers, and Comic Readers—a complete literacy program with something to interest every child.

Learning to Read, Step by Step!

Ready to Read   Preschool–Kindergarten
• big type and easy words • rhyme and rhythm • picture clues
For children who know the alphabet and are eager to begin reading.

Reading with Help   Preschool–Grade 1
• basic vocabulary • short sentences • simple stories
For children who recognize familiar words and sound out new words with help.

Reading on Your Own   Grades 1–3
• engaging characters • easy-to-follow plots • popular topics
For children who are ready to read on their own.

Reading Paragraphs   Grades 2–3
• challenging vocabulary • short paragraphs • exciting stories
For newly independent readers who read simple sentences with confidence.

Ready for Chapters   Grades 2–4
• chapters • longer paragraphs • full-color art
For children who want to take the plunge into chapter books but still like colorful pictures.

STEP INTO READING® is designed to give every child a successful reading experience. The grade levels are only guides; children will progress through the steps at their own speed, developing confidence in their reading.

Remember, a lifetime love of reading starts with a single step!

© 2023 Spin Master Ltd. PAW PATROL and all related titles, logos, characters; and SPIN MASTER logo are trademarks of Spin Master Ltd. Used under license. Nickelodeon and all related titles and logos are trademarks of Viacom International Inc. Published in the United States by Random House Children's Books, a division of Penguin Random House LLC, 1745 Broadway, New York, NY 10019, and in Canada by Penguin Random House Canada Limited, Toronto.

Step into Reading, Random House, and the Random House colophon are registered trademarks of Penguin Random House LLC.

Visit us on the Web!
StepIntoReading.com
rhcbooks.com

Educators and librarians, for a variety of teaching tools, visit us at RHTeachersLibrarians.com

ISBN 978-0-593-64726-4 (trade) — ISBN 978-0-593-64727-1 (lib. bdg.)

Printed in the United States of America

10 9 8 7 6 5 4 3 2

STEP INTO READING®

nickelodeon

Runaway Rocket!

by Elle Stephens
illustrated by Emi Ordas

Random House 🏠 New York

There is a space fair
in Adventure Bay.
It has a real rocket!

Uh-oh.

Chickaletta gets

into the rocket.

It takes off!

The rocket soars

into town.

The mayor asks Ryder
for help.

The Mighty Pups
and the Cat Pack
are ready!

Chase and Wild
follow the rocket.

It flies to a farm.
It almost hits
the barn!

They follow the rocket
to town.

It almost hits a van!
Skye moves the van
just in time.

Shade sees
the rocket's path.
It is going back
to the space fair!

Chase and Wild
are on the way.

Oh, no!
The rocket traps
the mayor on a ride.

The ride takes off!

Rory jumps
on the rocket.
She turns it off!

Leo helps it land.

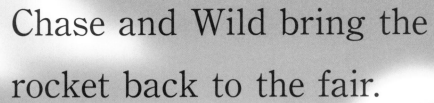

Chase and Wild bring the
rocket back to the fair.

The mayor
and Chickaletta
are safe.

Hooray for the PAW Patrol— and the Cat Pack!